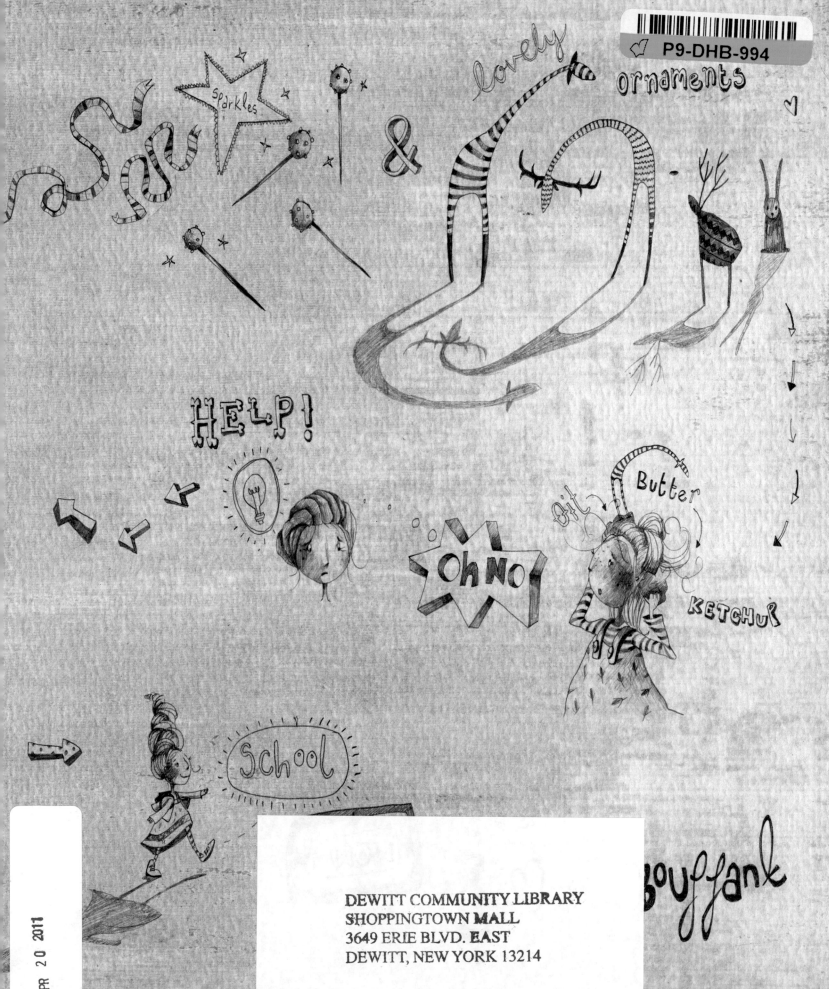

Big Bouffant

Kate Hosford

illustrations by
Holly
Clifton-Brown

Carolrhoda Books / Minneapolis

Carolrhoda Books
A division of Lerner Publishing Group, Inc.
241 First Avenue North
Minneapolis, MN 55401 USA

Website address: www.lernerbooks.com

Library of Congress Cataloging-in-Publication Data

Hosford, Kate.
    Big bouffant / by Kate Hosford ; illustrated by Holly Clifton-Brown.
        p.   cm.
    Summary: Fed up with the unbearably dull hairstyles of her classmates, Annabelle wrangles her
hair into a giant bouffant hairdo to be different—until her new style becomes the trend to follow!
    ISBN: 978–0–7613–5409–3 (lib. bdg. : alk. paper)
    [1. Stories in rhyme. 2. Hairstyles—Fiction. 3. Individuality—Fiction.] I. Clifton-Brown,
Holly, ill. II. Title.
PZ8.3.H7878Bi 2011
[E]—dc22   2010016385

Manufactured in the United States of America
1 – DP – 12/31/10

To Charlie and Andreas —K.H.

To Chloe and Megan —H.C.-B.

On the first day
of school, Annabelle sighed.
She looked around the room,
shook her head and cried,
"Ponytails and braids!
Ponytails and braids!

I don't see anything but **ponytails and braids!** This class needs some fashion. This class needs some fun. I'll find a hairdo to impress everyone."

She skipped back
to her house and
twirled in the door

as a picture of her
grandmother fell
to the floor.

Annabelle stopped
quite suddenly
to stare at
Grandmother's
marvelous
tower of hair.

"Oh please, Mom, please, can I have a **bouffant?**

A **big** bouffant is all I really want!"

"I don't want to look like all the other girls!"

Annabelle ran over
to the kitchen shelf.

"If I want a
bouffant,
I'll just do it
myself."

Butter

tomato
Ketchup

Honey

Mayonnaise

Oit

Annabelle smeared butter
and honey on her head.

She
p u l l e d

and she piled

until her face
turned red.

When she leaned
to the left,
her hair slithered right,

but Annabelle
kept styling with
all of her might.

She added in ribbons,
then sparkles and a bow.

She added in ornaments,
row after row.

She stood back and wondered,

"Is it too much?

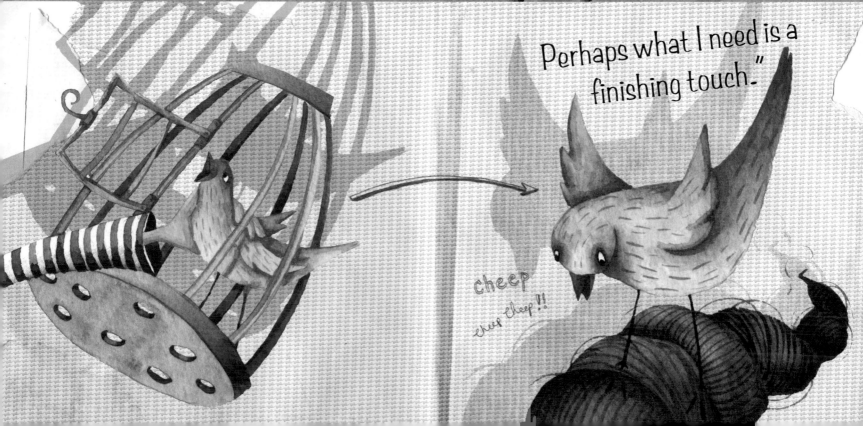

Perhaps what I need is a finishing touch."

cheep cheep cheep!!

But Annabelle's bouffant was beginning to melt.
"This is certainly the stickiest that I've ever felt!

After a shower,

several cookies,

yum yum yum

and a rest,

Annabelle decided on the plan she liked best.

"Please, Mom, could we make another bouffant?"

"I suppose," Mom said, "if you really, **really want.**"

On Tuesday at school,
when Annabelle appeared,
a lot of girls giggled
and a lot of girls sneered.

But Annabelle was happy with her brand-new style,
and she waltzed through the playground
with a great big smile.

On **Wednesday** at school, when Annabelle appeared,
just a few girls giggled and a few girls sneered.
Some girls told Annabelle, "We love your big hair!"

On Thursday,
the braids and the ponytails were gone
and the girls had bouffants—each and every one.

The boys filed in with their
hair combed tall,
and the teacher's bouffant
was the biggest one of all!

20 in

15 in

10

Katy

Annabelle
went home
and slumped
on her bed.

"My bouffant's so boring.
I want something new instead!"
She thought very hard with
her eyes closed tight.

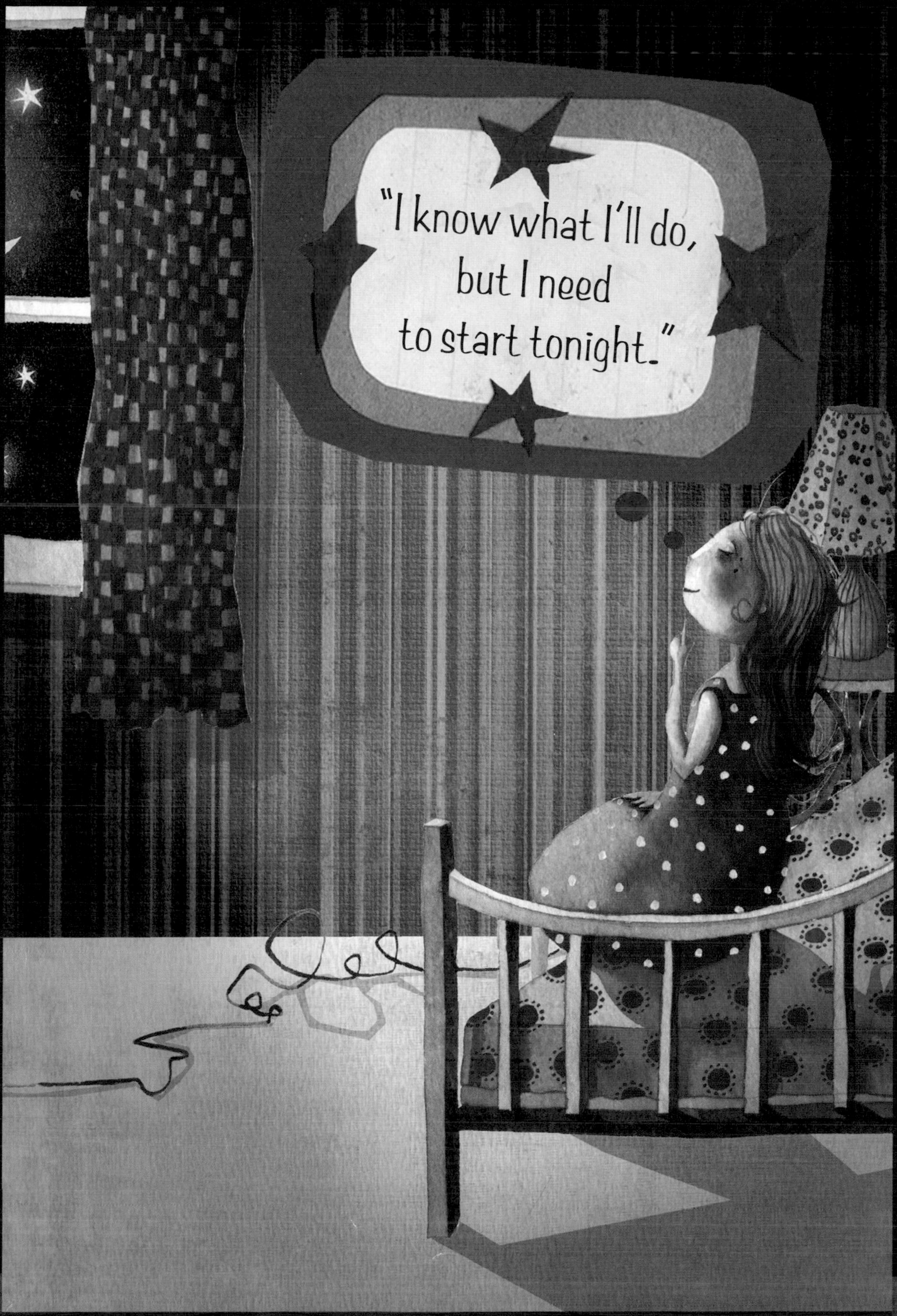
"I know what I'll do, but I need to start tonight."

She tiptoed
through the house

as she gathered
her supplies.

She'd be the queen
of fashion with her
next big surprise.

Her plan was a secret.
She wouldn't write it down.

On Friday, there
were ten bouffants . . .

but only one gown!

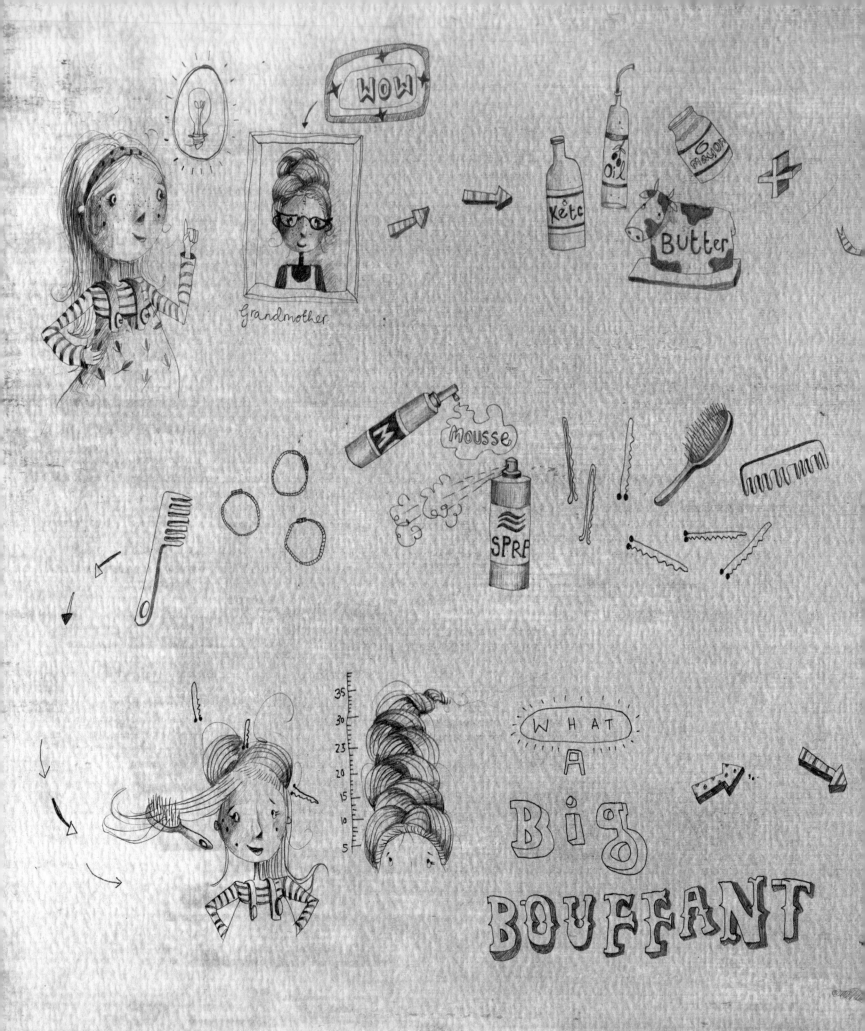